ROBOT SON

ROBOT SON

Robert F. Young

Lathehand approached the tek temple warily. It stood on a russet hillside, a row of golden maples curtaining its brusque facade. Above it the sky showed brisk and blue and clear.

He shivered. The morning was relatively mild, but the memory of the chill night and the frosty dawn was still with him, and even the warmly rising sun could not drive the memory away.

He moved forward slowly, keeping behind a stand of garnet-leaved sumacs. The frost on the grass had transmuted to dew, and the dew seeped through his thin sandals and numbed his feet. He felt the fear deep inside him, marveled that a tek temple should have inspired it. He should have felt reverent, not afraid. Tek temples symbolized good, not evil—

Or had, until the Tekgod had murdered summer: set the leaves of the trees on fire and drenched the world in daytime rain, coated the dawn grass with transient silver, filmed familiar ponds and puddles with brittle ice, transformed balmy zephyrs into bitter winds that raised tiny lumps on your skin and made you see your breath. And certainly, if the Tekgod was capable of turning, against his children overnight, his teks and tekresses were also capable, and their temples could no longer be considered as sanctuaries.

But, as representatives of the Tek Kingdom, they had the information Lathehand wanted—the why and wherefore of the Tekgod's action, and the location of the Temple of Heaven. Moreover, their temples were well-stocked with food, and Lathehand hadn't eaten for days.

The stand of sumacs patterned the course of a small brook that wound down the hillside. Halfway down the slope, the brook made a wide curve that brought it quite close to the east: corner of the temple. When he came opposite the corner, Lathehand dropped to his hands and knees and began working his way through the slender, elf-like trees. He kept his eyes on the ground, carefully avoided twigs and fallen leaves. The sound, as well as the sight of him, could provoke the attendant tek into ill-considered action, and Lathehand had no intention of dying just yet. He had faced death too many times these past few weeks, and he had developed a passion for staying alive.

The sumacs closest to the brook were more riotous than the outlying ones. They formed a garnet curtain through which it was impossible to see.

ROBOT SON

Lathehand parted the curtain carefully—and found himself looking straight into the cold gray eyes of a gold-robed tekress.

She was sitting calmly on the opposite bank, her legs folded beneath her robe. Sunlight limned her fair, full face, glittered on the U-235 symbol that adorned her skin-tight cowl. A paralyze pistol lay on her lap, its muzzle pointing, almost casually, directly at his forehead.

For a long time Lathehand did not move. The tekresses regarded him steadily, her slender fingers stroking the pistol as though it were a lovable pet instead of a deadly instrument capable of turning the human-body into a malfunctioning hulk of unfeeling flesh. Presently: "You wished to see me?" she asked.

He nodded. Numbly.

"Yes, Your Virginity," he said.

"You chose a rather circuitous way of going about it."

"I was afraid, Your Virginity."

"Why should you be afraid of a tekresses?"

The pistol still pointed at his forehead, but her fingers had ceased their stroking motion, lay quietly on her lap. Some of Lathehand's courage returned and he edged his body part-way through the curtain of leaves. "Why should a tekresses be afraid of me?"

Color touched her cheeks, lending them an evanescent softness; but it had no effect on her austere, watchful eyes. "In times of crisis, certain men react in certain ways," she said. "They plunder, they pillage . . . they rape."

For a moment Lathehand was speechless. Then: "You — you thought—"

"I watched you for almost an hour. You advanced—unorthodoxly —for a man bent on a religio-technological errand. Should I have, thought differently?"

"But Your Virginity! A *tekresses*! I did not, would not, dream!"

She looked at him intently. He had never seen eyes quite as gray and as deep as hers were. Presently she stood up, slipped the pistol into her robe. "No, I guess you wouldn't," she said. There was an odd note in her voice. "But you didn't answer my question," she resumed. "Why should you be afraid of a tekresses?"

He got to his feet and waded through the brook. She watched him carefully. Lathehand was not a large man, but his shoulders were wide, his limbs muscular. His hair was dark and disheveled, his young face hard and thin. He climbed up on the bank and halted several feet from her. "Because I'm afraid of the Tek-god," he said.

"I see."

"Why did he destroy summer?"

"I do not know."

He swayed slightly, giddy from hunger and the new knowledge that tekresses, as well as ordinary humans, could be something less than omniscient. "But you *must* know!"

She shook her head. "But I don't." Then: "You look hungry. Are you?"

"Yes, Your Virginity."

"Come with me."

Inside the temple, she led the way through the huge sub-ganglion chapel to the living quarters in the rear. Lathehand stared at the towering banks of gleaming controls rising straight up to the lofty dome-through which the morning sunlight filtered in nacreous splendor. The chapel was typical rather than unique; there were thousands of others just like it, situated at key points all over, the world, each linked to the master ganglion, in the Temple of Heaven; but it had been so long since he'd visited one he'd forgotten how awe-inspiring the works of the Tekgod could be. Then he promptly forgot again when he stepped into the automatic kitchen and saw the long row of gleaming food dispensers.

The tekresses dialed a vaaiumized breakfast unit and set it before him. He devoured the bacon and eggs hungrily, washed them down with the hot coffee. When she asked, "Still hungry?" he nodded, and she dialed sweetrolls and jelly, and more coffee. He leaned back finally, gave a long sigh, "That's the first food I've had since my flyabout crashed three days ago," he said.

"You should have known it's unwise to fly in unpredictable weather. Why did you leave your mech-town?"

"Because I was frightened, I suppose."

ROBOT SON

"If you'd really been frightened you'd have cowered in your mechanized habitat like the others. You were curious, not frightened. That's encouraging."

"Why is it encouraging?"

"That's a secret thought," she said, "arising from a personal attitude toward the Zeitgeist. I'm afraid you wouldn't understand . . . What do you plan to do now?"

He looked at her for a long time. He weighed the softness of her cheeks against the austerity of her eyes, tried to balance the fullness of her lower lip with the firm line of her chin. Finally: "That depends on you, Your Virginity."

Surprise widened her eyes. He saw her reach instinctively into her robe, "Explain yourself," she said, and her voice was so cold he could almost see her frosted words.

"I want you to take me to the Temple of Heaven."

The surprise in her eyes intensified, turned into disbelief. "And what do you expect to find there?"

"The Tekgod, for one thing. The way back to summer, for another."

"You're being quite presumptuous for a mere mortal."

"Am I, Your Virginity? I got up one morning and the grass was silvered with frozen dew. I'd never seen frozen dew before, and for a while I couldn't understand what it was. I went outside and it was cold. *Cold*. Before that moment, the word as applied to air had no meaning for me. Suddenly it had overwhelming meaning.

"The morning after that I got up and the sky was overcast and rain was falling. Falling furiously *in the daytime*, not softly in the night the way sane rain should, but *in the daytime*. I could not believe it till I went out and felt the rain on my face, and then I had to believe.

"There came a night not long after when die sky brightened blindingly at intervals, and the brightness was followed by deafening, demoralizing rumbles. More rain fell. The next day I noticed something else. The color of the leaves was changing. To red, to gold, to brown —to a thousand intermediate hues. And not only that, the leaves were detaching themselves, one by one, and drifting slowly to the ground . . . No, Your Virginity, I don't

8

think I'm being presumptuous in wanting to find the Tekgod, in demanding an explanation. I think he owes me—and the rest of mankind—an explanation."

"I think he does, too," the tekresses said unexpectedly.

"Will you take me to him, then?"

She lowered her eyes to her hands. They lay pale and immobile on the table. The long, sensitive fingers were tightly interlaced, and the fingertips were white. Presently: "Perhaps you are presuming a quality in me which I do not possess," she said.

"I'm presuming nothing. I'm merely asking a favor."

"The quality I had in mind was courage."

He stared at her. Her eyes were still lowered, still preoccupied with her hands. Finally: "You have a flyabout, don't you, Your Virginity?"

"Yes."

"Then let me borrow it and tell me the way I should go."

There was a silence. Then there was the whispering sound of her robe as she stood up, finally the sound of her voice. "I'll take you," she said.

Haze hovered over the land, and through the haze the gold and red and russet of the new season showed, in the unpremeditated patterns of woodlands, in the haphazard outlines of fields and meadows. Now and then the sapphire loveliness of a lake drifted by beneath them, and once they glimpsed the serpentine ribbon of a river.

The tekresses's flyabout was a one-man affair, and they were forced to lie close together on the horizontal pilot-bed. But, despite the severe limitation of space, the tekresses still managed to maintain an inch's distance between their prone bodies. Lathehand was grateful for that: he was not used to consorting with tekresses, and sharing a bed with one, even when the term was figuratively applied, embarrassed him as much as it indubitably embarrassed her.

But an inch was very little, after all, and it could not begin to dispel the sense of intimacy which the situation imposed. Lathehand found himself glancing at her more and more often, marveling again and again at her symmetrical profile, at the soft swell of her throat. He kept thinking of a statue he had seen once—a sensitive impression of a nude woman that somehow, abnegated the very sex it seemed to shout.

Presently she raised her eyes from the floor viewer, intercepted one of his glances. He noticed her long dark lashes, the way the golden hue of her skin-tight cowl intensified the milk-whiteness of her complexion. He wondered curiously what her hair was like: whether it matched the midnight darkness of her eyebrows, whether it was straight or curly, whether it was dull or bright.

Her gray eyes, probing coldly into his, disconcerted him, and he looked away. He culled his mind for something to say that would take the edge off his embarrassment. A question would be best. Tekresses were accustomed to answering questions, and he had any number of them to ask. "How could anyone destroy summer?" he said presently. "Even a Tekgod?"

"Strictly speaking, he didn't destroy summer. He simply deactivated the Meteorological Modifier and summer departed of its own accord, for the simple reason that the season wasn't summer at all—at least not in a meteorological sense, but fall instead."

"I don't understand, Your Virginity."

"You could hardly be expected to . . . The pre-tek period was deleted from the public mentors' tapes generations ago, and today only teks and tekresses are taught that there was a period in human history—a lengthy one—when men, instead of machines, worked, followed by another period when machines worked but had to be operated by men. Most of our present surnames are derived from the chief occupations of this machine-operation age, though our given names date back to a much more remote age . . . Anyway, weather control followed soon after the birth of automation and was integrated into the early Tekchurch as a matter of course. It seems fantastic, even to me, that there could have been a time when man had to accept the weather for what it was, had to endure its various and unpredictable moods; a time when months like January and June were associated, in the northern temperate zone, with the words 'cold' and 'warm'; a time when there were four seasons, instead of only one—summer, autumn, winter, spring—"

"What season is this?" Lathehand asked. "Autumn. The last phase of autumn, in fact. Winter is near."

"Is winter worse?"

"Much worse."

"Then why did the Tekgod deliberately bring about its return?"

She dropped her eyes. "I told you before: I do not know."

"But you suspect."

"Perhaps."

"Then tell me. I have a right to know."

"A tekresses is forbidden to discuss religio-technological matters with anyone who is not a member of the hierarchy," she said with sudden hauteur. "I've said too much already."

"I'm sorry, Your Virginity."

She acknowledged his apology with a brusque nod, and the conversation ended. When she returned her gaze to the floor viewer, he followed her eyes, saw that the Flyabout was passing over the ruins of an ancient city. Steel, over a period of 5,000 years, was as ephemeral as wood over 500; beams and girders that had once supported and held together fabulous tons of brick and mortar were now no more than occasional discolorations on crumbled masonry, and even the masonry itself had half-vanished beneath trees and vines and lichen. Lathehand had always wondered who had built the cities; now, in the light of his new knowledge, he understood that .they were products of the pre-tek period. Man had built them, not machines. The concept was staggering, and he put it out of his mind.

Beyond the city, the terrain changed from a gentle drift of fields and valleys to a sequence of hills. The flyabout had been traveling north all day, and the higher hills were covered with a strange white substance. In the distance, mountains showed, and here the whiteness was more pronounced, extending sometimes halfway down the slopes. Snow, Lathehand thought, wonderingly. Snow . . .

One of the hills caught his eye, not because it was covered with snow but because it was covered with something else. People. The tekresses noticed too, and dropped the flyabout in a wide spiral.

ROBOT SON

As the distance diminished, details stood out with corrective clarity: only the slopes of the hill were covered with people; the hilltop itself was reserved for a single figure—a man in an incongruous white robe. His arms were raised, and he appeared to be addressing the multitude with passionate earnestness.

Lathehand heard the tekresses gasp beside him, heard her voice: "*It can't be!* Even a paranoid old man wouldn't be so deluded as to think that—" Abruptly she bit her lip, and he felt the sudden pressure against his thighs and chest as she threw the flyabout into swift ascent.

At that moment the white-robed man saw them. He raised his arm till his fingers pointed directly at the flyabout's prow. Blue light leaped from his fingertips, and the craft began to flounder and lose altitude. The tekresses worked the controls desperately, but the ground rose up relentlessly, giddily, overwhelmingly. Then, at the last minute, the flyabout righted itself and settled serenely into the grassy hollow at the foot of the hill.

The tekresses's face was white. As white, Lathehand guessed, as his own face probably was. It was some time before either of them spoke. Then: "We'd better get out of sight," Lathehand said. "He might blast us again."

The tekresses shook her head. "I don't think he'll harm us."

"Then why did he knock us out of the sky? *How* did he knock us out of the sky simply by pointing at us?"

"I imagine he needed a miracle and was reluctant to deface the immediate countryside. We provided him with a convenient means for performing one."

Lathehand threw open the coping, climbed angrily out of the pilot-bed. "I don't know what's going on," he said, "but I do know he almost killed us, and without any provocation at all! I don't intend to let him get away with it."

The tekresses had climbed out after him. She touched his arm. "He's gotten away with it already," she said. "Look." Lathehand turned toward the hill. The men, women, and children covering the slopes were kneeling, their heads were bowed. The white-robed man stood imperially above them, arms folded, eyes uplifted to the sky. He was speaking, and his impassioned, vibrant voice rolled over the land:

"Is there one among you who doubts my identity now?" he demanded. When no one answered, he went on: "Once again I say unto you: My father is angry. In your pursuit of selfish pleasures, you have neglected him. You have taken his divine favors for granted and have given nothing in return. You have *lost* him, and now you must find him again—through trial and tribulation, through suffering and hardship; through me!"

The speech — or sermon — was over. The white-robed man started down the hillside, his audience making a path for him, falling in behind him when he reached the base. He headed straight for the fallen flyabout. When he reached it, he halted and folded his arms across his chest. He regarded Lathehand and the tekresses with dark, almost luminiscent eyes.

He was quite tall, and his bronzed face was strikingly handsome—the brow wide and high, the nose almost geometrically straight, the chin firmly molded. Lustrous chestnut hair tumbled in waves to his white-robed shoulders in chromatic harmony with his short wavy beard. His robe seemed to absorb the pale sunlight, reprocess it, and then release it in soft shimmering waves.

"Follow me," he said abruptly, and turned and strode away. The people trailed after him like mindless sheep.

The words had been spoken in a tone that contained no hint of command. Yet Lathehand felt compelled to fall into line, to follow unquestioningly wherever the white-robed man might lead him. He glanced at the tekresses, curious as to her reaction, saw that she had re-entered the flyabout and was systematically trying the controls.

Presently she climbed back out. "It's completely dead," she said. "We can never make it to the Temple of Heaven on foot."

"We can try," Lathehand said. "We've plenty of food . . . How far away are we now?"

"About two hundred miles."

Lathehand glanced at the sky. The sun was low in the west, disappearing rapidly into a brooding cloud bank. He lowered his eyes. The hills rolled bleakly away in all directions. Trees, standing in groups in the valleys and alone on the hills, looked dead, and some of them—the tropical ones scattered incongruously among the endemic oaks, maples, elms, and poplars—really were dead.

A wind was drifting down from the north. He felt its cold breath against his face. He returned his eyes to the tekresses. "What do you think, Your Virginity?"

"I think we'd better 'follow him' —for tonight, anyway. We can leave our supplies in the flyabout . . . Perhaps we can start out tomorrow."

Lathehand nodded. Then: "Who is he?" he asked.

"According to him, he's the Tek-god's son."

"Is he really?"

The tekresses sighed. "In a way, he is," she said . . . "Come, we'd better hurry."

*

There was a valley sleeping among the hills, a long deep valley scattered with trees, mottled with meadows, bisected by a brook. Poplars, their leaves yellowed by the first frosts, grew along the brook looking like huge stalks of goldenrod in the afternoon light: tall fall flowers with sturdy stems and pale, impromptu petals.

There was a settlement in the valley, and they started down the slope. The uniform dwellings were gray in the deepening shadows, their windows warm with light. People moved along the narrow, geometric streets toward a central square where the white-robed man was breaking bread.

Lathehand stared disbelievingly when they reached the square. There was but a single loaf of bread, but the white-robed man broke and broke, and the loaf never diminished. Not only that, the bread was rich and filling: Lathehand had been hungry, but his hunger vanished with the first mouthful.

He regarded the white-robed man with new respect, a respect colored with awe. Abruptly he heard the tekresses's voice beside him: "Look at them! The gullible fools! All of them have duplicators in their own houses and yet they are so influenced by a change of setting, by an unprecedented situation, that they interpret a technological commonplace as a miracle." She glanced at Lathehand contemptuously. "And you're no different!"

"But *he* has no duplicator," Lathehand said,

14

"Not ostensibly. But there's probably one hidden in his robe."

"Why should he want to hide it?"

"Because miracles create awe. Technological gadgets do not. The Tekgod, even in his dotage, is aware of that"

"Your Virginity, that's blasphemy!"

She paled slightly. "Perhaps it is," she said. "But I'm glad I said it.. . Here comes your savior now."

The white-robed man had finished breaking bread and was approaching them. "Follow me," he said again, when he came opposite them, and Lathehand took the tekresses's arm and they fell in behind him.

He did not pause till he reached the outskirts of die settlement. Then he turned suddenly and confronted the tekresses. "You doubt me, don't you?" he said

The white oval of her face stood out starkly in the darkness. But her eyes were clear and unafraid, her voice calm. "Yes," she said, "I do."

"I am the son of God," the white-robed man said. "I am the divine Repairman come out of the wilderness to reanimate your souls and to lead you back into my father's grace." He faced an empty plot of ground, raised his arm. "Let there be shelter!" he said, and a dwelling grew out of the earth. "Let there be light within!" Yellow radiance poured forth from doors and windows. "Let there be suitable furnishings!" Chairs and tables and couches took shape. "Let there be heat!" Steam condensed on the window panes. He turned to the tekresses. "You still doubt me?"

She was shaken. Lathehand, who was shaken himself, saw the slight twitching of her lower lip, the trembling of the hand she raised to her throat. But she said: "I'm quite familiar with matter transmission."

"Machineless matter transmission?"

"You have a machine hidden somewhere."

A pause. Then: "You will have all winter to look for it!" Abruptly the Repairman's voice rose, took on a shrill quality. "What are you doing in the company of a common male?" he demanded. "Why did you disregard my father's decree and leave your temple?" When she did not answer, he went on: "If you had evinced a vestige of the simple faith you see in the eyes of the people around you, in the eyes of your companion, I would have created you a dwelling fit for a tekresses despite your wanton behavior, despite your dereliction of duty. Now I will create you nothing. If your companion sees fit to take you into this, *his* dwelling, he may do so; but you will not enter it as a tekresses—you will enter it as an ordinary woman!"

The tekresses stood straight and still. Her white face seemed choked by the tightness of her cowl. "You haven't the authority to deprive me of my rank," she said.

"I have the authority invested in me by my father who is the one God and the only God and upon whose side I shall sit in the Temple of Heaven when the ravages of winter have brought his children back to an awareness of his omnipotence!" the Repairman shouted, and, seizing the tekresses's cowl in steel-strong fingers, he tore it from her head and ripped it to shreds.

He turned and strode away.

Scarlet usurped the whiteness of the tekresses's face. It was as though the Repairman had torn, her robe from her, instead of her cowl, and left her standing naked in the street. Her hair, a breathless mass of midnight, tumbled darkly to her shoulders, and she tried futilely to cover it with her arms as she ran sobbing into the newly-created dwelling.

Lathehand did not move. He wanted to move; he wanted desperately to run after the Repairman and beat him with his fists. But he couldn't. His awe of the son of God outweighed his anger.

He didn't know how long he stood there, listening to the tekresses's sobs, but his limbs were stiff from the cold and the sky was pulsing with stars when he finally threw off his inertia and entered the hut—

For it was little more than that: neat, white, uniformly heated, divided into two main rooms—but a hut withal. The tekresses was huddled in a corner of the front room. Her sobs had ceased, but her head was buried in her arms and her hands still tried unsuccessfully to hide her hair.

Lathehand closed the door quietly. He took a deep breath, slowly expelled it. Then: "I know next to nothing about the tek hierarchy, Your Virginity," he said, "and I would be the last to disagree with, any of the rules and regulations by which it operates. But it seems to me that honest beauty is a rare thing, in any of our lives, and that when we come across it we should not turn our eyes away from it, nor hide it, nor suffocate it . . . nor, above all, be ashamed of it, no matter what tradition says, no matter what convention dictates."

She did not answer him. She would not even look at him. Her arms were white and rigid against her temples, her hands pressed tightly upon her head.

"Your hair is beautiful, Your Virginity . . . "

Silence stepped into the room and sat softly between them. He saw her arms relax, drop slowly to her sides. He saw the artificial light touch her hair, disintegrate into a million microcosmic stars. Her eyes lifted to his. Once there had been ice in their deep grayness. He saw the last particles of it melt away.

She stood up, smoothed her golden robe. She did not speak. Lathehand stepped across the floor, opened the door to the back room, and stepped inside. It was identical, both in decor and appointments, to the front room. The Repairman, he thought wryly, was as sex-conscious as the Tekgod.

He returned to the front room, shoved the couch against the wall opposite the connecting door. The tekresses had not moved. "I'll sleep here," he said, not looking at her.

"Yes."

"He said you were no longer a tekresses," Lathehand went on. "His saying it doesn't make it so. To me you are still a tekresses and therefore inviolable . . . "

"Yes," she said again. He was perplexed by the tone of her voice.

It should have connotated relief, but it did not "The tradition you mentioned a moment ago," she said. "I—I wonder if you know *why* tekresses cover their hair."

"No, Your Virginity."

"I—I'd almost forgotten myself." She lowered her eyes to her hands. "It began millennia ago, when machines had women operators. A lathe or a drill press could be quite dangerous if the operator's hair became entangled in it, and because of this it became customary for women operators to wear head-coverings. The custom was discontinued when fashion brought about bobs and bangs and feather cuts; then, much later, when complete automation revolutionized our way of life and our way of thinking, it was revived and integrated into the early Tek-church. It has endured ever since, though most of us have forgotten its origin . . . " Abruptly she raised her eyes. "You realize, probably, that the only reason I'm telling you all this is to make myself feel better."

"I suspected you might be," Lathehand said. "*Do* you feel better?"

"A little."

He looked at her. She was standing in the doorway that connected the two rooms. Now that it was no longer surmounted by a cowl, her robe was suggestive of a golden dress. Her hair lay like jet silk on the golden swell of her shoulder. Her eyes were wide and luminous, the corneas pinkened from crying.

Her lower lip contrasted more sharply than ever with the strong line of her chin.

"Tomorrow we'll try to get out of here," Lathehand said. "If you want to."

"Do *you* want to?"

"Yes."

"Then I do, too." She turned and stepped into her room. "Good night," she said.

"Good night, Your Virginity."

She closed the door. Softly . . .

*

The world was white, and particles of whiteness sifted steadily down from the sky. Lathehand was frightened at first when he looked through the window, and when he opened the door and the dawn-cold struck him, he was shocked. Then, when he realized what the whiteness meant, he was bitterly disappointed.

He closed the door and stepped back into the room. "Snow," he heard the tekresses say, behind him.

"Yes," he said. He had not heard her enter the room, and he turned and faced her. He noticed instantly that her hair was different. Last night it had been tumultuously beautiful; now it was beautiful in a different way. It was smooth now, almost glossy, and fell to her shoulders in orderly waves. "I'm afraid we can't leave today, after all," he said.

"No."

"But the snow can't last forever. We'll leave as soon as it's gone."

18

"Whenever you say."

He felt uncomfortable, why he did not know, and he was relieved when a knock sounded on the door. Opening it, he saw a tall bearded man standing in the snow. "The Repairman's breaking bread in the square," the bearded man said. "Better hurry or you'll miss out."

Lathehand turned to the tekresses. "I'll get a double ration," he said.

"All right."

In the street, the bearded man said: "I'm Pressman."

"Lathehand . . . Thanks for stopping by."

"No trouble."

They walked in silence for a while. Then: "What are they like without their clothes on?" Pressman asked suddenly. "Not worth a second look, I'll bet!"

Lathehand came to a dead stop. The question was in poor taste, but it was a perfectly natural one. He had heard many jokes about teks and tekresses in his day, and he had laughed as heartily as anyone else. A normal person could hardly be expected to take chastity vows seriously. And yet, instead of the mild annoyance which the question should have evoked, he experienced an immense, overwhelming anger, and for an insane second he debated on whether he should kill Pressman by strangling him, by beating him, or by breaking his neck.

Pressman shrank away, his face ashen. "In Tek's name, what's the matter with you?" he gasped.

"Get out of my sight," Lathehand said. "Don't ever come near me again!"

Pressman almost ran down the street, disappeared around a corner. Lathehand followed slowly. The snow stung his face, cooling his rage, but his hands were still trembling when he reached the square.

The square was a "busy place for so early in the morning. Men, women, and an occasional child waited in a long line at the end of which the Repairman stood barefooted in the snow, breaking bread from his inexhaustible loaf. The sight of their warm clothing made Lathehand conscious of his thin leisure slacks and blouse, and he felt the wind more keenly. He also felt curious eyes upon him as he took his place in line.

When it came his turn, he asked for two portions, and the Repairman obligingly broke them off and handed them to him. Lathehand tried to hate

19

the man, but looking into those dark, deep and emotionless eyes, he could summon nothing but wonderment . . . awe. Deliberately he recalled the scene of the night before, and this time hate did stir in him. But somehow it would not rise till he was walking away with the bread in his hands, and. then it was too late.

"Wait," the Repairman said.

Lathehand turned.

"You have no warm clothing."

He saw the garments in the Repairman's arms, garments that had not been there a moment ago. He accepted them, was about to utter his thanks, when he saw that there was clothing for one person only. "But the tekresses," he said. "She needs clothing, too."

"I know of no tekresses in this community."

Lathehand swallowed. He knew what he had to say. "The woman in my hut," he said, hating himself.

Immediately more clothing appeared in the Repairman's arms. Lathehand accepted it before he saw how cheap and coarse it was, and when he tried to return it, the Repairman looked over his head as though he were not there. He almost threw it on the ground, but didn't. Clearly, coarse clothing was better than none at all, and equally clearly, coarse clothing was all the tekresses was going to get.

She made no comment when he handed it to her. She merely carried it into her room, then returned and ate bread with him. "Why is it so filling?" Lathehand asked when they had finished. "I've never tasted bread like it."

"It isn't bread: it's a condensed dinner camouflaged as bread . . . After all, we wouldn't be of much comfort to the Tekgod's ego if he let us waste away through malnutrition."

"You mean the Repairman's ego, don't you, Your Virginity?"

She looked at him quickly, glanced away. "Yes, of course. The Repairman's ego . . . Please don't call me that."

"Why not?"

"Even tekresses have names."

"You've never told me yours."

She hesitated a moment, then; "Mary . . . Mary Machine. I—I don't know your name, either."

"Joseph Lathehand."

A silence settled around them, a strange silence permeated with a quality that Lathehand could not at first identify. The room, with its simple furnishings, seemed to bask in a warm light: the chairs, the table, the couch—a far cry, all of them, from the mechanized appointments he was used to; appointments that anticipated your every wish, that entertained you, that worked for you, that adored you . . . But, certainly, simple appointments were better than none, and there was a refreshing honesty, a certain dignity, about a chair that did not follow you around like a dog, a table that refused to devise new delicacies to delight you, a couch that would not make up reassuring dreams to tranquilize your sleep. Suddenly Latheland knew what the quality was—

It was peace.

The snow fell for three days and three nights. Morning, noon, and evening, Lathehand went to the square for bread. At night he went to the square to hear the Repairman speak. Attending the sermons was not mandatory, but despite the weather, everyone in the settlement turned out. Everyone except Mary Machine.

*

The Repairman spoke of many things, but he spoke primarily of mankind's indifference to the Tek-god. This indifference, he said, stemmed from the average person's reluctance to accept the Tekgod as a real god, to relegate him instead to the position of a sort of supreme tek. This, the Repairman insisted, was sheer apostasy. The Tekgod was a *divine* being, and right now he was an *angry* divine being. The weather was a reflection of his wrath, and the only way to modify it and to bring about the return of summer was to come to him through his son and to accept him as a divine being.

Lathehand was bewildered. "I've never questioned the Tekgod's divinity," he told Mary Machine. "I don't think anyone else has. Why should he accuse us of a lack of faith?"

"Paranoia," Mary Machine said.

He was shocked. "But he can't be insane! He's *God!*"

"God or not, he has the symptoms of paranoia. And not only that, he's betraying another facet of mental instability: he wants us to fear him."

"But why should he want us to fear him?"

"For one thing, he's in his dotage. For another, he's apparently been reading history and has discovered that there were gods before him, gods who did not need to rely on technology for their divinity. Unquestionably, he's been reading about a certain god in particular, a god who—"

"But there's only one God," Lathehand objected. "There's never been another!"

"There have been many. The world is much older than you think."

Lathehand stood up, distraught. "You're a tekresses. How can you say such things!"

"I say them because they're true. As true as the Repairman is false."

"But he's the son of God! You believe that, don't you?"

"With qualifications."

"Then why do you say he's false?"

She dropped her eyes to her intertwined fingers. "I—I don't know," she said presently.

Anger touched him. "You're lying!" he said impulsively. Then; "Forgive me, Your Virginity."

"There's no need to forgive you. I was lying."

"Why?"

"We may be here for some time. I want to preserve your peace of mind."

"The minute it stops snowing, we're leaving," he said. "So whatever you have to tell me, you can tell me now."

She shook her head. It occurred to him suddenly that even tekresses weren't above stubbornness. "After we leave, I'll tell you," she said. "Not before."

He had to let it go at that.

*

On the fourth day, the snow ceased falling. When he awoke, Lathehand blinked his eyes at the unexpected brightness of the room. He became aware of a vague tightness in his chest as he hurried over to the window and looked out at the immaculate new world, and there was a strange instability about the floor. Presently he realized that it wasn't the floor that was unstable, but himself.

Other changes in his physical *status quo* manifested themselves as he dressed. There was a dragging ache in the small of his back; his limbs were heavy; despite the fact that the room was cool, he was sweating. But in his haste to get started, he paid no attention.

When he finished dressing, he knocked on Mary Machine's door. She was already up and dressed. "Pack as many blankets as you can," he told her. "I'll get our supplies from the flyabout."

"All right."

He started for the door. Abruptly the room spun, and he staggered. Nausea rose in him. He saw Mary Machine's white face swimming in the gray, swirling mist that reality had become, felt her arm around his waist. He marveled at her strength at she half-carried him back to the couch, and suddenly he knew the coolness of her hand on his white-hot forehead. He heard her voice:

"You're not going anywhere today," she said.

It was an old, old word, so old that it had nearly vanished from the language; so old that only a tekresses who had read too many ancient books would remember it at all—

Influenza.

The virus wouldn't have hit him so hard, Mary Machine told him—much later, when his delirium was behind him—if he had been living in the pre-tek age. But centuries of summer had undermined man's immunity to his oldest enemy, and the mild but elusive virus that had been capable of causing a three or four days' illness five thousand years ago was now an omnipotent entity capable of keeping a healthy person flat on his back for weeks.

For a long time Lathehand thought he was going to die. For a long time he wanted to die. His dreams were cesspools of fears and repressions whose existence he had forgotten. His waking moments were little better. What made them endurable at all was the reassuring softness of a voice he could never quite place, and the reassuring presence of a white face, framed in midnight darkness, that was the same, and yet not quite the same, as a face he had known in a far happier reality.

ROBOT SON

At the beginning of the second week, he began to feel better. Mary Machine read to him then—not out of books, for there were none, but out of her mind. She had an eidetic memory, and he would watch, sometimes, while she closed her eyes and searched for a phrase or a line mentally photographed years ago, and invariably be startled at the unexpected freshness her voice would give to an archaic turn or twist of thought.

The books she read to him were commensurate with his recovery. In the beginning, there was one called *Ivanhoe*—a romantic fantasy which he found difficult to understand because it was based on a set of values for which his own thought-world could provide no criteria. Much later there was one called *The Brothers Karamazov*, another fantasy which he found difficult to understand for the same reason.

Finally, there was one called *30 Pieces of Chrome*, and this one he had no difficulty in understanding because it had been written during the early years of the Tek-church. But, while, he could understand it, he could not accept it, for it was a blazing indictment against the Tekchurch and against mankind. From its impassioned prose arose the startling accusation that man, after a few half-hearted and much publicized efforts to reach the planets, had turned his back on the stars and converted his science into "a contemptible lapdog dedicated to the gratification of its master's every whim." The end result was the glorification of universal automation and the apotheosis of the supreme tek who, from a strategically located ganglion, held electronic jurisdiction over every sub-ganglion in the world, and through them controlled the operation and maintenance of the vast system of subterranean machines and reactors that supplied energy to everything from a household mentor to the Meteorological Modifier itself. The over-all result was spiritual decadence, the increasing reluctance of married people to accept the responsibilities of parenthood and the consequent falling off of the birthrate, an unrestrained indulgence in the physical pleasures of the moment because of the Tekchurch's failure to come up with new concepts of "heaven" and "hell," and the popular identification of the latter concept with boredom. The author, Mary Machine said, had been tried by the tek tribunal for heresy, found guilty, and given the radiation chamber.

24

After *30 Pieces of Chrome*, Lathehand's recovery was rapid. Soon he was able to walk around the room, and not long afterwards he was able to spare Mary Machine the humiliation of going to the square for bread. On his first visit, he was surprised at the smallness of the crowd, and then it dawned on him that the virus had not singled him out in particular, but had spread throughout the whole country.

When he got back to the hut, Mary Machine was missing. A note on the table said: *I'm at the Diemakers. Their child is ill.* Up till now, she had had nothing to do with their neighbors—a logical reaction in view of the fact that their neighbors would have nothing to do with her. Apparently the Diemakers had suffered a change in attitude, or, more probably, had adapted their attitude to fit their situation.

Curious, he went out into the street and inquired his way to their hut. The wind had shifted to the south and the snow was swiftly turning into slush and dirty water, John Diemaker opened the door. There were dark pouches beneath his eyes. "Come in," he said.

Lathehand stepped inside. A little girl lay on a couch in the far corner of the front room and Mary Machine was kneeling over her. The girl's mother stood to one side, crying.

"We thought she might be able to help," Diemaker said. "Tekresses know lots of things."

"Can't the Repairman do anything?"

Diemaker shook his head; "He was here. But all he did was look at her and turn away. I—I didn't know what to do—till I thought of the tekresses."

The little girl's moon-face was flushed, her breathing labored. Mary Machine's hand rested on the small forehead and she was speaking in a low, almost inaudible voice. Looking down at her, Lathehand caught her face in profile, and it was as though he were seeing her for the first time. Her face had intrigued him before because of its contradictions: the contrast between die full lower lip and the determined line of the chin; the clash between the austere gray eyes and the soft full cheeks. Now a new quality had appeared—a quality that eliminated the incongruities completely and brought every feature together into a supremely balanced composite that came very close to beauty. Perhaps as close to beauty as it was possible to come.

ROBOT SON

Lathehand couldn't identify the quality. It was too tenuous for him to put his finger on. But, watching her, he remembered suddenly the strange face he had seen during the delirious phases of his illness, and he realized that this wasn't the first time he had seen the new version of Mary Machine; that it had been her face floating in the mists of his nightmares, calming them and turning them into bearable dreams.

As he watched, standing there in the hot close room, he became aware of a difference in the background sound. The wind still moaned around the eaves, the mother's crying continued uninterruptedly, and the father kept clearing his throat at intermittent intervals as though about to voice a question he was afraid to ask; but beneath all those various sounds, the sound of the child's breathing had changed. It was even now, and quieter, and looking closer, Lathehand saw that the small moon-face was no longer flushed, that sweat no longer glistened on the little brow. The mother noticed the change then, and her sobs died away, and when Mary Machine stood up, she knelt at her feet and pressed the hem of the tekresses's robe to her lips.

Two patches of red appeared in Mary Machine's cheeks. She pulled her robe away, raised the woman to her feet. "I think she'll be all right now," she said, and turned and left the hut. Lathehand followed.

*

In their own hut, he said: "I brought out bread. Are you hungry?"

She nodded. They ate silently, facing each other across the table. After a while: "The snow's melting fast," Lathehand said. "Maybe we can leave tomorrow."

"If you wish," she said. "It's not what I wish that counts."

"Then nothing counts."

"I don't understand, Mary Machine."

"A woman can be many things: she is never one thing only. It's unfair to assume that the first person you thought her to be is the only person she is capable of being. You still don't understand."

"No," he said. Then: "Would you rather stay?"

She looked around the room, and he got the impression that for her the walls were no longer there, that she was seeing the whole settlement, perhaps the whole world. Presently: "Many of them are sick now," she said. "Many more of them will be sick tomorrow. And tomorrow and tomorrow. Is it right to leave them?"

"They're the Repairman's responsibility, not yours."

"It would be more appropriate if you said they're the Tekgod's responsibility, not mine. It would also be equally untrue."

"But what do you owe them? For weeks they've ignored you. For weeks they've made up obscene little stories about our relationship. Yes, it's true," he went on, when a blush darkened her neck and cheeks. "It's true and you know it's true!"

She spoke with difficulty. "Whatever they've said arose from the same frustrations and fears that have always afflicted human beings and probably always will. I have no right to condemn them for it."

"Then you'd rather stay?"

"Only if you do."

He sighed. "All right then. We'll stay."

For a moment he thought he saw a smile soften the corners of her mouth, but he couldn't be sure. He had never seen her smile before, nor heard her laugh—

It occurred to him suddenly that Mary Machine was a very unhappy woman.

*

The snow melted far faster than it had fallen, and the settlement became a quagmire of muddy streets. Then, one morning, the Repairman raised his arm and said: "Let there be flagstone walks among the houses and a flagstone pavement upon the square!" The problem was solved.

The influenza problem, however, was not solved. The epidemic grew worse, seemed to thrive on the warmer weather. More and more men, women, and children took to their beds, and when word of Mary Machine's curing the Diemaker girl got around, more and more people sought her out.

She was hardly ever home. Morning, noon, and night there was always someone who needed her, and she never refused them. Lathehand could not understand what powers of healing she possessed, but whatever those powers were, her patients invariably recovered. And it wasn't always a matter of touching their foreheads and murmuring a few words, either—though sometimes this simple treatment effected an immediate turn for the better. In the majority of cases she spent hours, sometimes days, at a single bedside.

Once, when she was employing the first method on an afflicted woman, the Repairman entered the hut. Lathehand, who was kneeling beside her, imploring her to go home and rest, saw him slip into the room and stand unobstrusively in the background. The dark, luminous eyes glittered oddly in the artificial light as they followed her every movement, and the expressionless face took on the hue of yellowed parchment. Several days later, Lathehand learned that he had used the same technique on another patient. The patient had died.

With the thaw, the ranks of the Repairman's followers swelled. The snow and the cold had convinced even the most skeptical that the change in the weather was going to continue unless they did something about it, and even the most stubborn that freezing in heatless houses would profit them nothing. Word of the Repairman's coming had somehow got around, and every day people poured into the settlement, beseeching him for bread and shelter. He did not refuse them, and the settlement overflowed till it covered half the valley floor.

Some of the incoming people had already been exposed to the virus; others were half-dead from it. And still they came, eager to see the Repairman's miracles, hopeful that he would restore the weather to its normal *status quo*. But, while they came to witness the Repairman's miracles, they stayed to witness the miracle of Mary Machine healing the sick.

She was a familiar figure on the streets, tall, hurrying, immaculate, and strangely beautiful, in the coarse gray clothes the Repairman had given her. A white kerchief covered the top of her head, but her hair spilled down in ritous darkness to her shoulders for everyone to see. People, when they met her, bowed and stepped aside. Some of them even made the sign of the atom on their breasts.

The Repairman, on the other hand, passed almost unnoticed among his flock. His nightly sermons were attended by mere handfuls of the faithful, and sometimes even they did not stay to hear him through. At first he gave no evidence that he resented the wane in his popularity. He continued to break bread in the square, morning, noon, and night. He walked the streets in the dignified manner that befitted the son of the Tekgod. Every so often, he performed a miracle or two. Finally he went so far as to move a mountain, but the performance faded into insignificance when, several hours later, Mary Machine performed the simple miracle of saving another human life. That night he failed to show up in the square with his inexhaustible loaf of bread and, later on, he failed to show up to deliver his equally inexhaustible sermon.

He didn't show up the next morning, either, or the next noon. That night, when he finally did show up—minus his bread but bursting with his sermon—he had a capacity crowd.

Lathehand stood with Mary Machine on the outskirts of the crowd. She had insisted on coming despite the fact that she had not slept for nearly two days. Fatigue had devastated the fullness of her cheeks, thinned her lips. Her eyelids were much too heavy, her eyes far too bright. By accident, his hand touched hers in the darkness and he was startled by the hotness of her skin.

"Mary," he said, "you're sick."

"No."

Suddenly she swayed, half-fell against his shoulder; but when he tried to lead her back to the hut, she resisted with surprising strength. "I'm all right!" she said, and the anger in her voice made him step back. Presently he realized that he was still holding her hand, and he dropped it hastily. The brightness of her eyes seemed more pronounced than ever: they seemed almost to glisten in the starlight.

The Repairman's sermon was brief and to the point: "Once again you have failed my father," he cried, "and once again my father is angry! There is nothing he cannot do for his children, nothing he would not do for them. But when they forsake him for a faithless tekress with the powers of a witch, his wrath is great. His discontinuance of your daily bread is merely the first manifestation of his displeasure. There are many more to come—unless you repent; unless you reject the false tekress and return to me, and through me, return to *him!*"

At first there was silence, then the scraping sound of feet on flagstones. People glanced covertly at Mary Machine, glanced quickly away. A murmur arose, gained in volume as it spread throughout the crowd. Abruptly someone shouted: "And if we do, will *you* heal our sick?"

The Repairman's face retained its undeviating impassivity, but the shrillness of his voice betrayed his fury, "Is that your answer?"

"Yes," someone else shouted. "What good is bread to the dead!"

"Then die!" The Repairman raised his arm. "Fall on them!" he shouted to the distant mountains. "Cover them!" he screamed to the surrounding hills.

The ground began to tremble. There was a rumbling in the distance.

"Wait!" Mary Machine cried.

The Repairman lowered his arm. Instantly the ground steadied and the rumbling faded away. She started through the crowd toward the center of the square, "Can't you see he's insane!" she said, when Lathehand tried to stop her.

"Then use your paralyzer pistol on him!"

She shook her head, freed her arm from his grasp. "It wouldn't do any good," she said.

He watched helplessly while she walked through the lane the people made for her. When she reached the Repairman she stopped and bowed her head. "What must I do?" she asked.

As usual, the Repairman's face provided no index to his mood; but again his voice betrayed him, this time not by shrillness, but by a pervasive purring note. "Luke Seven, thirty-eight," he said.

Without a word, Mary Machine turned, left the square, and started down the street to her hut. When Lathehand fell in beside her, she waved him back. "Trust me," she said, "and please don't interfere."

Minutes later she returned, bearing a basin of water. She set it at the Repairman's feet and knelt before it. Slowly, meticulously, she washed each foot and dried it with her hair. Lathehand watched numbly, forced himself to go on standing where he was. A gibbous moon showed above the lip of the valley and its silver rain glistened, almost glittered, in her dark luxuriant tresses. Presently he saw her stand up, her head still bowed. Suddenly he saw her fall . . . and he was running, then, forcing his way through the speechless spectators to her side.

He picked her up and carried her out of the square. Behind them the Repairman began breaking bread.

*

The southwind breathed its last breath and gave up the ghost, and the west wind came riding over the land like a furious Brunnhilde on a savage white charger. Snow fell again, not softly as the first snow had, but in slanted fury, in white and swirling gusts, spuming down from the hills and collecting in the valleys. The days were bitter with cold, and the nights haunted by the Valkyrie-voice of the blizzard.

Mary Machine made an ideal victim for the virus. Her lack of sleep and her overexertion had weakened her more than Lathehand had suspected, and he was dismayed at the rapidity with which she succumbed. Worst of all, while she could heal others, she could not heal herself, and there was no other Mary Machine available to come round and cure her by the sheer force of unselfish devotion. True, several of their neighbors did drop by and self-consciously offer their help; but their lowered eyes betrayed their insincerity. Lathehand turned them away.

Gradually he understood the reason behind their change of attitude. The Repairman had played his hand shrewdly, and even though Mary Machine had given the people back their bread for her act of humility, the nature of the act itself had destroyed their respect for her. And this, coupled with the falling off of the influenza epidemic—strangely coincident with the drop in temperature—had restored the Repairman to his former position.

Day after day, night after night, Lathehand sat by her bed. For a long time she was delirious, and during this phase she seemed obsessed by a coming event which she referred to as the "transfiguration." He humored her, though he hadn't the remotest notion of what the term meant. As nearly as he could understand from her vague ramblings, the "transfiguration" was a change which was supposed to occur in the Repairman's physical make-up at a prearranged date and in accordance with the historical episode upon which the Tekgod was basing the analogous "ministry" of his son.

Once she said: "We never should have let him stay in office for so long. We should have known that senility was inevitable, and we should have known that when he reverted to childishness, he would mindlock himself in his

31

ganglion tower and make some childish gesture calculated to attract attention to himself. And most of all, we should have known that a childish gesture on the part of a man with illimitable power could result in the destruction of the world."

On another occasion, she said: "I sometimes think that in clothing mere maintenance men and women in the robes of priests and nuns and in forcing them to forego their sexual need, we have only succeeded in stultifying the ideal we tried so desperately to sanctify."

On still another: "The events that fashion ideologies sometimes reoccur, and the ideologies themselves follow soon after. Basically, history is a panorama of repetition."

And once, in the middle of a dark and lonely night, she shocked him by crying out: "Let him kiss me with the kisses of his mouth: for thy love is better than wine! . . . I am a rose of Sharon, a lily of the valleys . . . The voice of my beloved! behold, he cometh, leaping upon the mountains, skipping upon the hills. My beloved is like a roe or a young hart . . . I was asleep, but my heart waked; it is the voice of my beloved that knocketh, saying, 'Your hair is beautiful, Your Virginity . . . '"

Lathehand lacked an eidetic memory, and even if he had had one, there would have been no books in his mind. He had never seen one.

But, in common with mankind, he had certain experiences which he had never forgotten, and when Mary Machine's eyes cleared again, he told her of his life in the mech-town that had been his birthplace: of his mentors and their stereotyped lessons, of the vague shapes of the two pleasure-seeking people whom he had been taught to regard as his parents; of stalking deer in the animation gardens and bringing them down with his deactivator rifle, and then activating them again and watching them run brainlessly away; of his various exploits in his flyabout and of his various exploits (expurgated) with women . . . and as he talked, the conviction grew in him that he had no right to talk at all, that in all his insipid life he hadn't done a solitary thing worth recounting to someone else. But if Mary Machine was ever bored, she gave no sign; in fact, there were times when he could have sworn that she was absorbed in his every word.

Presently he realized that she was getting better. Her forehead seemed almost cool now, when he touched it, and there were vestiges of color in her cheeks. But she was strangely nervous, and her nervousness did not dissipate even after she was strong enough to walk. She questioned him again and again about the Repairman's activities, and insisted that he attend the nightly sermons in the square.

He complied. Once again the Repairman was talking to a capacity audience, and his voice, vibrant with a sort of hysterical expectation, rose above the winter wind in strident overtones: "Soon you will see my father in me, see me resplendent in his shining glory, transfigured from a, mere mortal to a true son of God! And then the wrath of my father will rise to its glorious zenith, and the hills will come tumbling down, the mountains will tremble, the skies will darken and rain will fall, and the rivers will rise and cover the earth. Only those of you who believe in me shall survive!"

With each sermon, the hysteria in his voice built up more and more. At last the date for the great event was revealed: it was to transpire on the morrow. Everyone, men, women, and children, were to be ready at dawn to accompany him into the hills. Those who failed to do so were to perish in the coming flood.

Mary Machine was still weak, but she insisted on going. Dawn broke, gray and lowering. The wind was still from the north, harsh and piercing. Lathehand took her arm, and they blended with the forming crowd—with the Diemakers and the Oilers and Welders, with the Shearmans and the Toolmakers and the Metters—and flowed with it, in the Repairman's wake, out of the valley and into the hills.

The Repairman chose the highest hill of all. He ascended it slowly, and with vast dignity. When he reached the summit, he turned and faced the people covering the slopes. Then he raised his eyes to the heavens and spread his arms wide.

The minutes tiptoed past on tiny, soundless feet. The crowd was silent, its multiple faces white. Mary Machine's face was whitest of all, and Lathehand saw that she was trembling. "I had to do it," he heard her murmur, "A mad god is worse than no god at all."

Someone in the crowd gasped, and Lathehand raised his eyes to the hilltop. A change was taking place in the Repairman. He had begun to glow as though an eternal brightness, hitherto repressed, were seeping outward through his skin, through his robes. The glow increased, became a radiant, pulsing red, turned slowly to yellow. Someone screamed. A man standing some distance from Lathehand, fainted. The yellow radiance brightened relentlessly to white. It became apparent, then, that something was wrong. The Repairman began beating his body with his hands, as though the brightness were unbearable. Suddenly his robes flashed into flame, disintegrated. The Repairman, naked, was definitely not a man. His skin started to flake, turned to ashes and drifted to the ground. The white radiance turned to blue. The Repairman's face blackened, peeled away; metal mesh glittered where it had been. A single agonized scream rushed from the lip-less mouth, briefly rode the winter wind. There was a blinding puff of smoke, and abruptly the Repairman was gone.

Lathehand felt Mary Machine sway against him and he caught her in his arms. "Take me to the top of the hill," she whispered.

He led her through the shocked crowd. She was crying. On the hilltop, they paused beside the small mound of smoking ashes and blackened metal parts. She took a deep breath, waited a moment, then turned and faced the multitude. She straightened her shoulders. Her rich voice warmed the clear cold air:

"Go home to your mechtowns. The Tekgod is dead . . . *For, lo, the winter is past, and the rain is over and gone—*"

And suddenly the winter wind became a summer breeze, the sky brightened to blue, and the sun broke through the last absconding clouds.

*

"When I was a little girl," Mary Machine said, "I wanted a doll. My mentors told me that wanting to play with dolls was an atavistic yearning, and they refused my request. So I made one."

They had opened the windows of the hut and the warm wind blew through the room. Outside in the street, happy people were passing in the sunshine,

"It was quite an unusual doll," she went on, when Lathehand made no comment. "So unusual that, when my mentors called it to the local tek's attention, it was interpreted as my call, and I was immediately enrolled—confined would be a more accurate term—in the nearest tek convent. Naturally, the first thing they did was to take the doll away from me. But before they took it away, I had a great deal of fun with it.

"It could walk, talk, see, and hear, but in addition to that, it was a sort of a mechanical projection of my self-image. Wherever it went, I went too; whatever it saw and heard, I saw and heard too; whenever it spoke, it spoke with my voice. I was so closely allied to it electronically that I could actually feel its pain, and if someone had destroyed it while it was activated, I would have been destroyed along with it.

"Wanting to play with dolls is not a yearning confined to little girls only. Old men in their second childhood can experience it too . . . The Tekgod's 'doll' was a much more complex mechanism than mine was: it contained an inbuilt matter disintegrator, an inbuilt matter duplicator, and an inbuilt matter transmitter with a receiving radius of at least sixty feet. But essentially it was the same as mine: if you destroyed it, you destroyed its creator also." She dropped her eyes abruptly to the table where her white fingers lay tightly interlocked. "I didn't want to do it. But someone had to, and I was the only one with the opportunity."

"But you didn't destroy the Repairman. It destroyed itself."

She shook her head. "I knew that the Tekgod would, sooner or later, try to prove the Repairman's godhood beyond any doubt, and since he was following the pattern of an ancient episode, there was little doubt but that he'd employ a technological version of the 'transfiguration' contained in that episode. So when I washed the Repairman's feet in the square, I shorted one of the 'transfiguration circuits' in its heel. It was a simple operation and occasioned no pain, but even if it had, the Tekgod was so engrossed in his own self-idealization that he probably wouldn't have noticed; When he finally did realize that I'd spotted his subterfuge, it was too late: the 'transfiguration' was already taking place. And of course, when he died, his mind-lock on the ganglion door collapsed, and the Temple of Heaven teks were able to enter and reactivate the Meteorological Modifier.

"He'd shown signs of mental instability before, and we've been afraid for years that something life this might happen. Yet we were reluctant to take him out of office because such an act would have been unprecedented. Traditionally, tekgods serve till they die, and then the Tek Council elects a new one from their ranks. So all of us waited instead of acting, and when you finally shamed me into action, it was too late. The Tekgod's paranoia had already become critical, and his 'doll' was on the rampage . . . And yet, for all his madness, he tried to give the world what it needs the most—a new Christ."

"A Christ?"

She nodded. "But of course he failed. He couldn't endow his 'doll' with qualities he himself lacked. The Repairman was a hollow Christ, a Christ without compassion, without altruism, without maturity."

Lathehand was looking at her. "A Christ, then, would be a person unusually strong in those three qualities."

"Yes."

"Would a Christ necessarily have to be a man?"

She was startled. "I—I never thought about it that way before," she said. "Perhaps not."

He continued to look at her. Abruptly she stood up and walked over to the door. Bewildered, he went over and stood behind her. "I am not a Christ," she said.

"You could be one."

Suddenly he saw that she was crying bitterly. "Can't you see, can't you understand, that before I am anything, I am a woman?" she said. "The Tekgod freed me from one sexless prison; now you're trying to lock me in another. Why? Am I hideous to look at? Am I an animated statue with stone breasts? . . . Or is it because you're not a man."

It was as though she had slapped his face. He seized her shoulders, spun her around. He kissed her savagely, tried to bruise her lips with his own . . . and lost himself in them instead. The sunlight pouring through the doorway turned her tears to drops of gold. Her hair was a soft summer's night. He reached up and touched it wonderingly—

"Your hair is beautiful, Mary Machine," he whispered.

EPILOGUE

It is one year later. The new Tek god, alarmed at the continued decline in the birthrate, has decreed that all citizens return to their native mechtowns so that an accurate census can be taken. Joseph and Mary Lathehand have returned to the town of Joseph's birth.

They have landed their flyabout on the outskirts and have entered the town in search of a place to sleep. Mary is great with child. But the town is crowded with travelers and all of the stopovers are full, and the best they can do is a stable which the owner has convened into a makeshift apartment.

During the night, Mary cries out. Towards morning, a child is born, and a resplendent supernova rises in the east . . .

www.ingramcontent.com/pod-product-compliance
Lightning Source LLC
Chambersburg PA
CBHW050919120626
46552CB00004B/1650